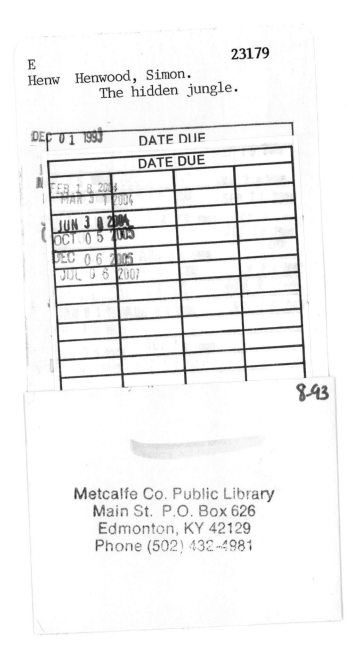

THE
HIDDEN JUNGLE

THE
HIDDEN

SIMON HENWOOD

Farrar · Straus · Giroux

New York

JUNGLE

Copyright © 1992 by Simon Henwood
All rights reserved
Library of Congress catalog card number: 92-3039
Published simultaneously in Canada by HarperCollins*CanadaLtd*
Printed in the United States of America
Designed by Martha Rago
First edition, 1992

To
Nick Maland
and
Wes Adams

For the last seventeen years, Mr. Pinn had lived at 26 Amelia Street. Things were pretty much the same in his apartment as the day he moved in. That's the way he liked it.

Mr. Pinn looked out of his
window. All he could see were
buildings and more buildings.
Except . . .

... today his view had changed. On his windowsill there was a young tree in a pot. Its trunk was sturdy and its leaves an emerald green.

Now, every evening, Mr. Pinn would hurry home from the office to see if the tree had grown.

Sure enough, day by day, it grew and grew. Soon the tree was too big for the windowsill, so Mr. Pinn moved it onto the roof.

Now that the tree was exposed, it needed more care. The dust and the dirt from the traffic below covered its leaves, and gusts of wind shook it to its roots. Mr. Pinn was surprised how much work was involved.

One day, Mr. Pinn discovered that
several of the leaves had turned brown.
Soon more followed, and the tree
began to wilt and die.

Mr. Pinn was upset. The tree just didn't like
the roof and all the noise and dirt and smell.
But then he thought of a place where
the tree might be more at home. A place
where there were plenty more trees.

Mr. Pinn looked out of his window.
All he could see were buildings and
more buildings.

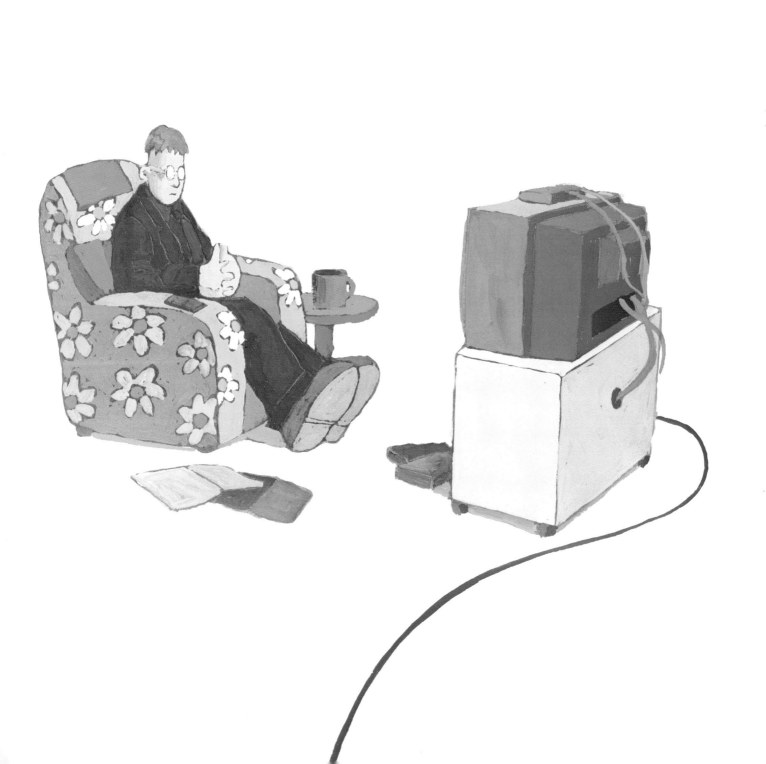